STARE INTO THE LAKE

DANIEL CHECHICK

Edited by: Yair Ben-Hur
Translated by Dr. English
Cover artwork by Tom McCloskey

DANIEL CHECHICK

Printed Worldwide
First Printing 2022
First Edition 2022

10 9 8 7 6 5 4 3 2 1

Edited by: Yair Ben-Hur
Translated by Dr. English
Cover artwork by Tom McCloskey

STARE INTO THE LAKE

TABLE OF CONTENTS

1.

It's dangerous to describe reality as it really is, Adam wondered to himself as he held onto the ink pen that seemed to be writing on its own, detached from the fingers gripping it. In those suspended moments, he looked at himself without any real grasp of reality, and they served him as a clever ruse against the existential anxiety that had intensified in him over the last few years, since that lover of his abandoned his world swiftly and without any explanation, like a person fleeing from terror.

He asked himself what part he played in said distancing every day, whether it was really better for him to flee it as a natural defensive step. But the more he questioned, the deeper he would find himself diving into the silence hiding in the depths of the lakes.

A fragile sense of helplessness wrapped him in a painful embrace that wouldn't let go, and was relentless in the face of these types of questions, until he closed his eyes and recalled the loving words of his mother, who did well to plant the thought in the fields of his soul that "the entire range of emotions is exposed to you in this life, from those that envelop you the most to those that paralyze you the most, yet you will forever be the deciding factor in it."

Those internalized words of hers would sometimes serve as a life raft for him, a reassuring confirmation that the vibrations of anxiety also had a place within the range of human emotions.

For many months it seemed to him that the colors standing out in his internal being were especially melancholic and dark, like dying flowers. He was desperate to find evidence of new buds of existence within his sinking turmoil. Had someone looked at him from the sidelines, one would see his eyes giving in to his sadness in a congruence that completed the magic circle, until a small twitch came to his face and from it a thought formed, especially hidden and exciting. It was a thought that supposedly contradicted itself, and only existed within him by way of a miracle.

How can I describe the emotions within me in these very moments, as my soul is present in the obsession of longing for earlier times that cannot be found?

These inner voices were unclear, and thus he asked to say a few words to clarify it for himself.

How can I know who I am and what I feel now, when all is influenced by my thoughts and my past?

Within all that, he unwittingly told himself – without even noticing – that he was foreign to himself. Having a hard time finding the words to express his emotions in those very moments, one might think his body was active in reality but his soul was not truly present; similar to him bringing his eyes close to the mirror and seeking to smash it to bits out of a hidden yearning, wishing to restart life without the impression of his old love so imprinted upon his soul.

That lover of his, she who was nothing but a familiar emotion whose existence was lost, became his soul's greatest object of desire, since her existence was singular proof for his good and familiar world, the one his heart had been longing for the entire time. "Had it not been for that love of mine, how would I know that I existed? Is she not reliable legal evidence that I existed?" he asked with his ink words, painting his recognition on yellow pages.

Within these kinds of thoughts, many years after their breakup, he started documenting countless memories in his being, which no longer existed, like someone asking to determine in his soul whether he himself might be a reliable witness to his own private existence, though deep inside he knew that it was nothing but a trick he operated on himself, since humans are not qualified to affirm their own existence but forever exist through the eyes of others.

These kinds of abyssal thoughts churned his guts, since he was gripped with trembling doubt as to his private existence in those times. And that was how he wrote down his emotions:

"They say you were a child and do not even have any memories,

They say you loved, but forgot her gentle voice

They say words, but who really knows?"

Just like that, without noticing, in his relaxation-seeking soul-searching, Adam was seeking her familiar gaze for many days, between the multitudes of people who were nothing but an ocean, swallowing him and nullifying his feelings in public. Her absence from external reality actually turned his soul as a storm would, and it seemed the memory of her face staring at him – so etched into his memory – made him search for her with such intense longing that he could picture, in his mind's eye, the gentle routes in the paintings of her eyes, in which he so loved to lose himself. His sight uncontrollably bounced to those who passed him by, out of that hidden yearning to meet himself in a loving space, where he could give himself over to being him, through a serenity-filled closing of his eyes. He wished to know that he had a place in the world, just as he had in those early days, in those memories he so longed for, but his determined walk through the crowd only made his desperation more present in that attempt to hold on.

He would sometimes take solace in that he did not carry her spirit inside him as an internalization all on his own, that she was probably finding his presence in the veins of her soul as well. The war of these internal thoughts turned into a daily routine, and became especially intriguing for him since there was no clear solution in sight.

~ ~ ~

Within that absurd reality, Adam started mailing anonymous letters to random addresses where he asked people "How do you know you really exist?", in the hopes of finding a firm grip in the whirlpool of existence that surrounded him, from which he could not escape. But aside from one letter that came back and said, "This is a question that has no answer", no one replied. He took comfort in the fact that the mental suffering he carried with him was not just within him, but within another person in the world as well, an "other" who also carried this sensation. Deep inside, Adam secretly thought that this "other" was no less than all of humanity.

Anxious thoughts such as these, which seemed to pierce him from the outside, intensified his need to scribble what might be questions, in which he described the sensations from the bottom of his soul, perhaps even from behind his thoughts – an attempt to find some firm ground within the experience of existence, even if it was full of question marks. The main thing, so he hoped, was to avoid that sense of helplessness in which the anxiety overwhelmed him to the point of tremors of terror.

Despite his aversion to said anxiety attacks, he knew that they sometimes were quality evidence that he indeed existed and was not just imagining his reality. These types of suffocation sensations, he wondered as he caressed his bearded cheek, seemed to be bursting out of the unconscious without any prior warning, undoubtedly expressing his most basic and core pain, making his soul present here and now while channeling the fabrications and illusions he had draped himself with during the journey of life, to escape and avoid truly meeting himself.

At the same time, it became ever so clear to him that anxiety did spare anyone, and was common even in the souls of the masses. But in those extreme moments where he would meet himself in crucial tremors of the soul, he would hold onto the thought that he was the only one in the entire world dealing with such powerful lonely emotions.

~ ~ ~

Adam was no different from those common grains of sand that made such efforts to calm cry of meaning that burned inside their souls. He was therefore active in the social world, and took pride in being an educator at school. He was excited to be part of the young human creation unbound by the limitations of the common exclamation marks of its older population. His pride as an educator was witnessing the developing ability of his students to ask questions, rather than them humbly accepting the required knowledge transferred unto them. His students knew that they could always ask questions and talk about any topic in the world, without reservation, with naïve humanity and wide-eyed curiosity.

Thus, he sought to create a safe ground for investigation, a pleasant space for his young loved ones, perhaps as he'd never experienced himself during his unstable childhood. Deep down in his soul he certainly believed in a religion that did not exist anywhere, the religion of questions.

Adam knew that despite all his efforts as an educator invested in human creation, it was not enough to hold onto relaxation and caressing sensations over time. His emotions uncontrollably ranged, back and forth, between the terror and the exceptional within him. How hard it was for Adam to consciously internalize that despite all his vigor, actions and meaningful roles, he had no power to control even a bit of his soul and emotions which sought to break through. It seemed that was only a childish wish that would never come true.

While walking within the masses, he did well to search the eyes of the "others" for that which they held onto in the guise of life's steady, and understood – by guessing – that all their actions in their active lives were but colors with which they chose to scribble, like concealing and repressing the darkening anxiety pulsating within them. It seemed they saw the reality of their lives within the distortion of the nullifying drug.

He would sometimes imagine malicious, almost diabolical thoughts in his mind, in which he would surprisingly scream at those passing him in the streets, right into their very souls, in complete surprise in order to scare them so that they would also be filled with the dread he held, just so long as he knew he was not the only one who had to deal with it. These screams were obviously only directed inward, into himself, since he was not yet brave enough to express his terror in public, but there was also power in those false illusions, or a hidden enjoyment in recognizing his capability to create an effect in the souls of others, all so easily. He often believed that all a person needed to live was imagine a certain capability, even if it was diabolical. *Such thoughts,* he would wonder to himself while sipping coffee at the pedestrian mall, *must certainly be common among all people, and even their smiles express another extreme.* Yet he was barely aware of his own existence, which was why it was pleasant for him to exist through those thoughts about said strangers.

~ ~ ~

Adam's feet pulled him to a nearby corner of a garden, where he looked at a boy and girl smiling among themselves as he could no longer do. The look in their eyes was like a creation his soul had forgotten. He looked at the gentleness of their emotional gazes and wondered to himself: "I once held onto their emotions, didn't I?" He bit his lips as if jealous, but also due to a chill that intensified along his long arm. "They are now touching the edges of life, so beautifully they don't even know it," he said to himself, this time outside his thoughts but in an actual silent whisper, as if applauding in gratitude.

He sat next to them on the ground and listened to the range of sounds that emerged from their loving smiles, like a scientist researching old memories. Yet each sound of their love was private and different than anything he'd known in his own world, since he realized in the flesh that each love was a new creation within the entire spectrum of emotion.

"There's no trace of my old love, she might not even be alive anymore, but how greatly present is she in my mental veins?" he asked, but there was no reply. This religion of questions was extremely active in the factory of his gentle soul. Men encountered many questions in their daily lives, and there were only a handful of real answers to be found, so much so it seemed that existential alienation was a requirement for human life.

At least the love of others is not foreign to me, Adam decided in his soul, in a bluntly envious thought since the lovers were behaving rather rudely in displaying their happiness in public, as if there were no wretched souls like him to notice and secretly wish to steal an embracing sense of gentleness, as a remedy for their dwindling lives.

Adam sometimes felt like someone who was about to give in to the endless thoughts that threatened to burst in his mind. Within his soul he somewhat enjoyed that ability to go deeper, like a fountain of thoughts he could dive into. He would suddenly smile to himself after managing to distill his love and clarify single thoughts, as there were very few people before whose very eyes he could express the deep darkness of his light. He would often walk around and document his fleeting thoughts in his notepad, so as not to forget himself, since that was how he proved his existence.

As he left the knights of love, he somewhat detached from the sense of alienation clinging to him in his jealousy of others, who were active in their lives, and in his mind's eye the image of Guri appeared, a true friend he had known from their days together at the religious school. The two were scheduled to meet at their favorite café, on the street corner, where they could overlook the masses.

They would always sit there at noon, a time when people would chase their own tails with speedy walks and serious expressions, as if holding onto a direction in life so that God forbid they would not have to deal with the anxiety burning in their souls. In that hunting hour, they could both willingly get lost in made-up life stories about said strangers. People who knew, deep down in their hearts, that no one would notice their absence had they never been born, and were capable of containing said bluntness between them, like a child's secret, but with such modesty that they could even project this thought onto their own souls, since they knew well the power of randomness.

He sometimes thought to himself how great was the grace in a childhood friendship that lasted a lifetime, since this uncommon experience was a similar testimony to his existence in so many shades. Guri was perhaps one of the only people in the world who knew him inside-out, as if they had a silent agreement that they could express their existential masks before each other without the sin of shame.

Their gazes intersected outside the café, and they shared a loving embrace, a "memory embrace" as they called it, a kind of one-time recognition that they were worthy of everything they were – from your terror to your exceptional. They sat at table number 7, with a painting of Heaven to the right, in which they found new meaning each time they looked at it.

"How are you, Adam? How's life treating you these days?" Guri asked, aware that his formulation was his soulmate's favorite.

Adam gently smiled, as if appreciating Guri's question that had multiple probable answers, not as the masses tended to ask when the required answer was always the one that helped them quickly go on without running into difficulties that would disrupt the comforting illusion.

"These are complicated days for my soul," he started telling him. "Malicious thoughts are taking over. Thoughts of longing for different times, times that no longer exist. It scares me very much."

"Are you still in mourning?"

"Mourning? No... I'm simply living. Is life mourning?"

"Some of it is... perhaps most of it. I don't know, this is a question worth looking into. It pains me that you've had these feelings for quite a long time, a few years now," Guri leveled his eyes at Adam and sipped his coffee.

"Can't a person mourn? Perhaps I'll be that way for an entire lifetime!" he berated him with contained anger. "I sometimes feel I see the world without the complete range of colors, as if there's no blue or green. Can you imagine that?"

"I think you can't see anything but black now," he gently smiled.

"Oh well… I've become an expert on living life in the black, isn't that creative?"

"Real creative! I know you, though, you find inspiration in the abyss of life, where your soul paints the most beautiful paintings."

A real wizard of words that guy is, Adam thought to himself as he breathed heavily. "I'm afraid I'll forget everything, afraid that one day I won't recall who I was in different times. I'm afraid to disappear in the damned lake of forgetfulness, afraid of being forgotten. I don't want all my beloved memories to be gone, and moreover – I wouldn't have her forget me," he said in an exhaled flow.

"Ahh… you are afraid to die…" said Guri.

"I'm afraid to die… am I not already dead? Perhaps I enjoy putting myself to death in all these thoughts? Only a man lost and in pain, submerged in sadness, can paint and create."

"You really didn't used to paint thoughts as well," Guri recalled. "But that's still no reason to give in to sadness, and for so many years. You must accept the state of affairs as is. You hang onto the past too much. The past is dead, my friend, nothing else could be more so…"

His last words play over and over in his thoughts. "Is the past dead?" *It seems the past is the only thing that lives in my world. My entire being is a history of thoughts, cellars of longing. Dead?! Nothing is dead here. Only the present is dead.*

"You are brave in your feelings. Not everyone is brave enough to die in the present. I think you're enjoying this daily death too much, see? It seems you can't let it go; this is your certainty now."

There's nothing like criticizing the philosophy of a loved one, Adam thought. "Your words pierce my guts, you should be a psychologist for humans, those out there who need to hear that they're enjoying losing themselves, right?"

"I only want you to not get lost, that's all. You least of all. These people outside, they mean nothing to me, but you… should you get lost in your thoughts of loneliness, I could no longer get lost with you, as we've been travelling our whole lives. My inner loss with you is the only certainty I have in my life," Guri said, and his eye sockets welled up with urgent red colors.

"You know it's an ever-moving cycle," said Adam. "But your ability to love me in these extreme moments is an affirmation that it's worth living."

After sharing a friendly silence and letting the words set in and soften their hearts, the two got up and said goodbye with a tight embrace, and disappeared into the masses in an immediacy that radicalized and displayed just how rare the human connection was.

How nice it is for a person to undress his thoughts before a soulmate, Adam wondered as he walked home after a long day of internal occurrences. The ability to express his thoughts hidden in the safe and gentle space, was the cure for love that was not common among the masses, and his heart was grateful for it many hours later.

~ ~ ~

Without paying any special attention, another day sought its finality. The lights grew fewer, and the night took over the windows. Adam lay alone in bed and attempted to silence his haunting thoughts to no avail, since his soul had become a thought factory that would not let go, like leeches digging into the depths of the stomach, able to remind one that they had been a fetus. His eyes focused on the candle flame heating by the side of his bed, and to the paintings of his imaginations came a picture of love in which he saw the shadows of his fingers caressing the gentle cheeks of that loved one of his, and the secret kisses following the peaceful hugs. Sweet memories made pleasant sensations surface through his body.

"In a lack of love, man turns the image of life around, from one edge to the next, just like orphancy" – he was reminded of one of his old sayings from his notepad. He suddenly started thinking about his clinging to memories of love… as if it were a remedy to his existential anxieties, wondering whether or not it was right. Therefore… what was the only remedy to anxiety in the souls of people other than the sense of love they were able to share between them? And as they touched and held onto these divine emotions, they managed to make the trembling existential questions redundant, even for a few minutes – it was, after all, a trick whose beauty was only revealed in the absence of that loved one of his. He had now encountered the trembling of his soul on a daily basis, without any adequate remedy.

After blowing out the candle and trying to deal with the darkness within him, his wriggling soul did not allow his eyes to rest in gentle serenity, and Adam cried with a stifled and fearful voice, as if secretly realizing that perhaps his greatest suffering in recent years did not derive from the abandonment of that loved one of his, but from the fear hidden in his soul that everything would be able to leave him, and that there's nothing he can do about it.

That living anxiety threatened his being, even though he couldn't always clarify it for himself, since it was enchanted and had pierced him, bursting into his soul when he wasn't aware of it at all. These kinds of powerful turmoil forced him to deal with his darkest places, which he hid so well from himself while hanging onto worlds that were external to him, and now he had no choice but look at his distress, directing his gaze forward with no escape route.

Adam lay down, and inner voices poured out of him in a colorful image of anxiety… as if begging to prove themselves to him, from within his own entity, how lost is the cause – this chase to fight the sanctity of randomness – he thought to himself, asking to shut his being off and enter a dream.

~ ~ ~

The illuminating sun warmed Adam's cheeks, and his eyes opened to a new day's morning. Every day that passed only heightened the sense that the world was indifferent to the stormy dealings of humans; everything kept going without lingering. *I gladly woke up, but I could have also not woken up*, a thought jumped into his head.

He immediately started getting ready for his workday at school. Before doing so, he went down to the basement of his house, out of an external force inexplicably and obsessively demanding to peek at evidence of ancient love. Living memories of pictures were kept in an old and dusty closet no one claimed, so much so that he sometimes dared question their credibility.

Adam looked through the old photo albums and was overwhelmed with his own emotions, frequently gasping when looking at his own eyes, which seemed to be lacking the existential anxiety he carried with him on a daily basis in recent years. From looking at their joint photos, he would anticipate additional imaginations burnt deep within his soul.

Adam smiled to himself at the absurdity, since all these only made his absence more extreme. "Dead, nothing else could be more so" – he was reminded of Guri's words, and told himself: *How nice it is that I can at least live that which has died.*

The stories from the photos made time stand still for many minutes. As he arrived at the bus stop, he found that he was late. People gathered around him at the stop until an old man suddenly arrived, who one might guess had been tall in his prime, but the burden of life had forced him to wrinkle by bending downwards, and perhaps that was why his eyes emitted a child-like curiosity for everything happening around him. The old man's casual demeanor caused Adam to envy him somewhat, as one who had already made peace with himself despite the hardships of life.

The hunched-over old man did well to lift his hand up, as if getting ready for the last fall, and as he randomly met Adam's gaze he turned to him and spoke. "I've never seen you here at the stop, are you new?"

"Me? No… I was just late this time. I'm here every morning."

The old man looked at him. "I guess I've never noticed you," he said.

"Look at that," Adam said. "You didn't notice me, and perhaps… I didn't notice myself for quite a while as well."

"What? You didn't notice yourself? Wake up, young man, this life goes by quickly. Fail to notice and you'll find yourself at the end of the road. You'll see… well, the bus is here. See you later," the old man blurted out with a puzzling smile.

Adam sat at the end of the bus and looked ahead to the old man who was speaking to the driver. It seemed the two had known each other for some time.

How wonderful set habits are, they certainly create a warm sense of security, Adam thought to himself as he stared at the baby stroller that held a brand-new world in it, a masterpiece that had yet to grow accustomed to any single thing. *Here is one nearing his death and another who has just been born – and I'm not certain which one of them I'm closer to.* They were both probably holding onto the sensation of life.

As he stood at the classroom door, the students stood up, as was the custom. He gestured to them with his hand, and they sat down.

Adam asked how they were, and to ask a question that was well-hidden within them, such that was neither polite nor acceptable to ask.

The silent children smiled amongst themselves in embarrassment.

A girl sitting next by the large window raised her hand and caught Adam's attention, while others seemed surprised that she of all people – the shy one – was suddenly so eager to take part in this type of conversation.

"Please," Adam told her with a gentle smile, stretching his open palm to her as if trying to instill a sense of security in her. She lowered her gaze in an attempt to stabilize her thoughts into a realization, and a few seconds later looked at the class and said: "I feel what I want to say is clear in my gut, in my inner senses, but I'm afraid I'll never be able to put them into words. I'm afraid no one will ever be able to understand me. Too many things come between what I feel and what even my mother can understand. Say… say I now pinch my own hand, it hurts. But no one knows how much it actually hurts. No one knows how I feel when I long for things. Everyone can attest for themselves… and that is… scary to me, it very much scares me that no one can ever feel what I feel."

Adam was fascinated by what the girl had said. He looked at the faces of his students, who were also charmed by her words that echoed within them and therefore avoided bursting out with frivolous replies, like a herd without a shepherd. The students were silent as a result of meeting the unconscious, a thought that probably also existed in their souls even though it had never risen to shape and color.

The class' lack of response did not serve as a balm for the girl's soul, whose cheeks began to redden as though sinning in shame. Adam felt in his flesh that he had to carry the sensations of the girl within the nullifying silence, and turned to her to say: "I'm proud to be the educator of a girl who can express words like you can. Very few people are able to make them heard, even towards themselves." Her gentle eyes began to stabilize and amplify at Adam's caressing words. A turmoil of this kind was so very foreign to all those who did not often express themselves in public. Suddenly she started to feel a pleasant warmth down her back, sensations that calmed the heartbeat seeking to escape the embarrassment, and flashes of confirmation that her thought was humane and magical, like a child being recognized by others for their abilities.

Adam looked at the softening of her anxiety and acknowledged the meaning of words to human souls, lost in chasing their attempt to get to know themselves. His gaze towards her, especially his words spoken in her ears, made him think how few were the words he himself had heard as a child , and how much he longed for them.

"You're actually talking about the experience of being lonely," he suddenly said. "We're all here together, in class, but each of us experiences their soul alone. No matter how many words we speak to describe it, no matter how scientific the evidence may be for the level of pain – one still experiences oneself on one's own. Is that where you were going with it?" The girl nodded, but Adam didn't settle for that and wanted to strengthen the 'religion of questions' in the eyes of his students. He immediately asked if there were other students in class that identified with that honest thought their classmate had expressed. Many hands were raised, almost involuntarily, an innocent acknowledgment in the fragile humanity of people.

After a few moments of silence, one of the students sitting in the front row lifted his hand and asked: "If we agree no one can understand how we really feel… does that mean we ourselves will never understand how others feel?"

The shy student burst out a reply, sensing that said student had continued her initial thought but added and described more advanced stages of her self-exploration. "Yes! It's like each of us is a certain color and there are only specific shades, which might be slightly similar, but eventually each of us is a separate existence that others can come close to but not actually touch. I'm not sure whether that stresses me out or actually makes it easier for me."

Adam, who smiled within himself at the philosophizing of his students in their self-exploration, looked at the class and asked: "Have you ever felt like someone actually saw you?"

The class was silent in a sort of helplessness that awaited an answer from up high, but Adam asked them to embrace this question in their lives for the near future, so they could meet themselves within its question as an emotional experience in their world rather than from teaching.

In conclusion, everyone agreed that they would like to keep deliberating the thoughts whirling in their souls, with the knowledge that sheer expression of this type of words in public served as a significant education on the essence of people and their existence.

These thoughts are not easy for young people, Adam thought to himself, inwardly agreeing that these kinds of life lessons had to come in small doses so they could be dealt with. Within all that, he wondered whether he might be overdoing it in his educational way, and should perhaps slow down the exposure of his students' inner desires before themselves.

These types of questions followed him as he left school, but in the personal brainstorming he also gave rise to a claim that engulfed his spirit: "I'm not dictating any path or view to them, they're the ones expressing themselves from within themselves. I'm only enabling them to have a safe space to express their humane sensations."

The conclusion of his thoughts also led him to wonder how great the distance was between his evaluated abilities as a humanist educator in the face of the difficulties he dealt with, so distant from himself, in his existential longings for his old soul, the one he so yearned for. That soul of his, with that loved one of his, suddenly seemed like fictional characters from a book thrown into the trash, since no one needed it anymore... as if there were depictions no one could identify with anymore, and were therefore shredded as if they'd never existed. In the depths of his awareness, he knew that the power of his loneliness in these very moments necessarily attested to the depth of the impression imprinted on his soul by that first love.

Within that, Adam continued to walk the paths of his thoughts on his way to the bus stop. His curious look drifted to the trees that had colorful birds who found a home there, resting on their branches. *All the birds in the world find a home while people search forever*, he thought to himself.

He occasionally found himself walking without invasive thoughts. It was a simple human experience of existence, and even moments of humble joy came from the lack of a storm, but once he recognized the face of the old man at the end of the road, he once again came to his own, like a man waking up in terror.

"You remember me now, right?" he asked.

"Remember you? Who are you?" the old man replied as he looked up without a shred of embarrassment.

"You met me this morning at the bus stop..."

"I'm warning you, young man, get away from here. Spare me your emotional distress, you're a stranger and so you will remain!"

Adam didn't understand how it was possible. How had his existence disappeared in an instant, within mere hours, with such violent and demeaning speed? *Perhaps the old man forgets everything... perhaps the old man forgets himself, everything*, thought Adam, *perhaps he is putting memories to death. But how is this possible? It seemed that the bus driver knew him this morning, it seemed that they knew each other, really knew each other. Perhaps that driver was nothing but a foreign soulmate helping an old man deal with his own foreignness? Still… how could he have forgotten me? It cannot be,* he shouted into his soul. *It's one thing to forget everyone else, but he only met me a few hours ago… has he already forgotten? How could he have forgotten my being so quickly?* Perhaps this was the way of humans, to keep going at lightning speed without answering or visiting the cemetery of the lake of memories.

This existential attack came from the depths of his soul, increasing his dizzying heartbeat, immediately causing him to shake in body parts he'd had yet to encounter in his world until then. His eyes began to darkened as though there was a screen of blackness, blunt and incurable terror, only giving into it without choice. He felt his soul caught in a powerful and tumultuous whirlpool that caused his body to fall to the ground, flaccid. The hot ground scorched the joints of his hand, and the old man, who was troubled by his foreignness until a minute ago, approached him with forced concern. Had God witnessed that absurd situation, He certainly would have wondered how strange humans were.

The old man lowered himself down to his knees, shouting for other people to help him. His hands started pounding

Adam's pale cheeks as if trying to revive him and inject some color into his transparent soul. It seemed that in those moments Adam was in a world of good, and an ancient divine silence enveloped him, just as he'd probably felt before he was born. The terrifying sounds of the ambulance were heard approaching from a distance, while additional strangers arrived like curious hyenas to look at the old man guarding Adam.

How fascinating it must have been for them to look at the unfortunate moments of others. What great rejoicing must be building up in their hearts that they were not currently in distress, but rather the other now desperate to be saved.

Adam certainly couldn't hear the wails of the crying girl who was out of her mind, since she couldn't contain the reality in which a person was standing up and suddenly falling without any grip. An older woman who could no longer stand the shedding of her tears held her in an attempt to calm her down, and said: "He'd probably been sick for a long time, it's the human way." Others tried to guess what had happened in an attempt to find evidence of a reason for the existence of events, but to no avail, since their words only made their lack of knowledge more extreme.

An ambulance arrived and the paramedics approached the old man.

“Did you see what happened, sir?”

“I didn’t see a thing, he simply fell.”

“Did he say anything before he fell?”

“He asked me if I remembered him, but I can’t remember anyone.”

2.

Adam's body lay in his sickbed while his soul traveled his dreams, to strange and faraway places where there were colors he'd had yet to see and emotions that exceeded human experience. His delusion was so addictive that even his consciousness, seeking a grip back onto reality, begged to prolong this enchanted trip. These tender moments were common to all people, as absolute evidence which expressed the extent of the gap between the power of the emotional experience and the harsh reality to which they valiantly fought never to return.

Reluctantly and submissively, Man wakes up to reality as if surprised, as if love was stolen from him. The shame of missing out prevents people from hearing these types of thoughts between them, but Adam, who had started to wake up with a troublesome headache, held onto that thought down to the bone.

Even when awakened to the reality of life, his soul always yearned for the imageries of different lifetimes. Mystical tricks of that kind were a fringe field of expertise during the lifetime of anyone who dared commit to the emotional experience so much that they'd lost themselves within it.

Adam didn't understand where he was, and started to probe the side of his bandaged head with his fingers. The bandage was small – a reason to calm down.

Perhaps something happened to me while I wasn't myself?

Perhaps, for the first time, I also fell outside the depths of my spirit? he asked himself.

He suddenly felt a chill running through his entire body. *Maybe these are Mother's caresses? Maybe strangers are, in their anxiety, seeking to touch me, blocking my soul from escaping?* he thought.

Those deep voices, coming from within him without any preemption as if bursting from the unknown, came in complete contrast to the sense of warmth that evolved within him as he lay in bed and looked at the vast white hospital room.

Beds are quite comfortable for human beings, whether you're sick or still lack the courage to admit you are, he thought to himself. The windows next to his bed seemed like a minimized painting where he saw a tree swinging and some clouds, in which he could not make out any imaginary characters. As he looked to his left, he saw the figure of a man sitting on the bed, holding his own pillow in a loving embrace. From his silent expression he imagined that his mouth hadn't uttered a word in many years, in the manner of monks. This wasn't religious practice, though; rather an acceptance of the ignorance of people who could not process the expressions of his soul.

Adam looked at him with envy and started to wonder how many other patients were stored inside this hospital's box-like rooms, and all over the world, while admiring the imagined number which was certainly in the millions. So many people wanted to rest, yet they called them sick. So many people honestly sought to express some internal human scream while being silenced with pills and confined structures, only because none had the patience to hug them. Stifled tears stood in Adam's eyes; he was so moved that he tried to understand and describe the world within itself, and now he suddenly saw it from without as well, an innocent humanity which wasn't obsessively holding onto common masks. For a few moments he thought he had been exposed to a rare loophole in God's creation, as if discovering a deep secret everyone was trying to hide.

The man appeared frozen, like a large stone that hadn't moved in many years. He seemed like someone who had absentmindedly determined that he was desperate to be parted from his yearning to be understood, and therefore reduced the expression of his turmoil in his apathetic facial features. Adam found himself hypnotized by that man's demeanor and his attempt to guess the entanglements of his soul. After a few minutes of staring at him, Adam imagined their honest conversation, which would certainly aim to expose their most blunt thoughts, since they were unwilling to lie to themselves.

One might think the silence of the hospital served as a cure for many people, as they were first and foremost free to clearly ponder the meaning of their lives, without the numbing noise of reality forcing them to always give in to existential meanings that weren't their own. That forced halt is sometimes a person's only chance to look at oneself without any bias, out of the loneliness that makes us see things as they really are. In those moments, Adam thought how much he was in need of a loving embrace to envelop him until he could feel another heartbeat. He immediately copied the man's actions and also absentmindedly held onto a pillow, as a balm to his soul, and at the same time began to grow angry at the view of the world and thought to himself: *what if people received a loving embrace in their time of need instead of all those soul-distorting pills that this industry limitlessly gives out? Is the doctor the messenger of God, as is commonly regarded, or are they the messenger of the public doing everything within their power to avoid having people scream their souls out in the streets?* So he invasively thought to himself.

"People flock to the hospitals in droves, secretly seeking someone to eventually pay attention to them, to treat them well and see them in their adulthood – with guilt-free and childlike devotion – so much so that they can hear loving and comforting words about them when dealing with a world in which the principles of randomness and helplessness beat so loudly. I sometimes feel like everyone I've seen, from the day I was born, spends their time looking for their parents, seeking comfort or love until the day they die, disguised as routine."

His conflicted and uncensored words obliged his soul to look longingly and without choice at all those cracks of existence in which people spent their lives without even knowing.

The volume of silence heard by those kinds of patients intensified the melody of the private words, which each would have heard within them; yet sometimes one could hear a heart-wrenching scream severing the illusion of peace, and it seemed that even this had no reason or source, but was simply concealed in a hidden corner of the heart until it erupted uncontrollably. The doctors and staff would stress out and recoil each time the silence was broken, fearing that one might hurt oneself or, God forbid, terrify the other patients. They'd immediately run around searching, making sure no one overstepped the boundaries of submission.

Just like in real life, they would immediately oppress those who dared speak out in an unacceptable manner. The silence returned with one precise action and the doctor went on to call in all the rooms, until he met the open eyes of Adam, and made his way towards him with a sensitive and empathetic smile. It seemed he was quite skilled at that.

"How are you, Adam? How are you feeling?"

"A little better, resting has done me well. Did anything major happen to me?"

"You're steady, but it seems you've undergone a severe anxiety attack."

"A severe anxiety attack? That's nothing new, I've never had a mild one."

The doctor smiled as if to acknowledge the truth. "You might be on to something. Still, your medical history never mentioned you helplessly falling to the ground and losing consciousness, certainly not from an anxiety attack. We should look into that further."

Adam started to think how this time was different, compared to all those anxious moments he'd known in his world, but had no answer for it.

The doctor came closer to Adam's face, as if seeking to give him advice. "Look, Adam, we ruled out any concern of epilepsy or other neurological issues in our tests. It seems to be an emotional experience, and not an irrevocable one. There are many patients in this hospital in severe condition, people we have no way of really helping other than maintaining their physical existence. I recommend starting therapy, I'm sure it'll relieve the emotional overload you're experiencing."

"Thank you, Doctor, I appreciate it," said Adam.

The doctor turned to the man on the other side of the room and suddenly looked back at Adam, as if surprised to see the two patients hugging their pillows. He instantly wondered how many of his patients needn't be under his responsibility at all.

~ ~ ~

Adam was mesmerized, looking at the clouds that never ceased to move gently towards an unknown destination for many hours. Smiles began to be painted on his face, like a child allowing himself to give in to the experience of play by holding onto the happiness that was almost impossible for an adult. Had the doctors looked into Adam's soul in this moment of life, they certainly would have determined that his acknowledgment existed in a space that had neither time nor will – a sort of self-healing trick yet to be made ready for scientific abstraction. It was so strange to discover, while daydreaming and being spiritually absent, that Man is able to commit to such a caressing sense of existence. The doctors would've certainly then determined that "the person is awake; too awake."

An open palm gently and suddenly rested on Adam's left shoulder, as if trying to pass along an encasing sense of home. It was Guri's hand. At that moment, even before shifting his look towards him, he thought it was an uncommon regard from God, from a human touch so simple it could often save people's souls.

"Adam, my friend! How are you feeling? It took me a while to get here, I apologize for that."

Adam started to return to reality. He was astounded that he'd managed to forget himself while strolling through the clouds. It seemed he had lost the ability to articulate himself as he dove into his friend's kind eyes. His heart held onto the excitement and appreciation of having a loving gaze to turn towards in that emotional turmoil that had struck him over the last 24 hours.

"I'm... I'm glad you're here, you have nothing to be sorry about. How do I look? What are my eyes telling you?"

"You seem fine. I talked to the doctor earlier... he said you're going through a crisis. Something emotional..."

"Yes... I thought this war would remain within me, but here, you can see my soul falling apart. My defenses can't withstand the might of life's attacks..." Adam said, concealing a smile. "But know that it's good to give in... the soul hints at it a thousand different ways, begging for that cessation. It begs so hard it sometimes screams, forcing you to give in to its cry.

And you can probably see the colors in my eyes, they seem clearer than ever, don't they? Look closely."

While looking closely into his eyes, Guri came to a decision, without understanding how impressive the experience of anxiety and crying was for Adam, as if it were an internal act of grace from a soul forcefully trying to shake off and purify itself of the toxins inscribed into Adam in his harsh reality. The eyes would clear out after a few hours of bright red colors outlining the tremors of crying, and one's powers of enlightenment would return to stand out as someone who had given himself exceptional love.

"You seem more balanced, closer to yourself... as if you've touched a specific point that was hidden and forbidden," Guri told him.

Adam closed his eyes as if attempting to cuddle some close words, but immediately let out rational ones for fear of being overwhelmed by his emotions.

"Balanced? I don't know about that. Perhaps I feel as if I exist more here now. In some twisted way, maybe hospitals are meant to bring a person back to their most primitive form, like an opportunity to reevaluate existence, even to enjoy being able to relieve your bowels in the restroom."

An awkward silence spread between the two, as though expressing an earthly humanity of existence from which they could not escape. “It’s nice to be grateful, even for that which is most animalistic,” Guri said, happy to discover that an optimistic observance could also be shared in times of great pain. After a few moments of compassionate silence, he asked his friend: “Still, what makes you shake so much you pass out while others don’t?”

“You know me… I still can’t come to terms with the possible death of my memories… the absence of that old soul of mine I so yearn for.”

“I feel your pain right in my flesh, especially since I’ve borne witness to most of your soul’s memories from back in our childhood. It was you who agreed that I see you in so many shades… I can look back on moments of life that even you have forgotten at any time. We are each other’s emotional storage of presence.”

“Does that mean you’ve also witnessed all those characters and masks we’ve shed over the years?”

“Yes, our absence also exists as a memory… after all, we’ve touched on so many colors, each time a bit differently… some would say we’re a little bit different every day, and perhaps it's inevitable that we'll be somewhat strangers to ourselves... a kind of painful truth we have nothing to do but live with; but still, see how beautiful our witnessing of it is. Generally... it seems that love is a collection of testimonies between people."

"My doctor doesn't philosophize with me like that. He asked me to see a psychologist; he probably doesn't want to get attached to strangers like me."

"And what do you think of his recommendation?" Guri asked, hoping to get an answer.

Adam diverted his gaze to the window, as if wishing to delay his response. "I'm afraid to express my emotional tempest to a stranger. It is, after all, so exposed."

"Perhaps it's the other way around? Maybe you'd be capable of being above and beyond what you know about yourself thanks to their foreignness?" Guri asked.

"You have a beautiful mind, Guri. Your questions make me miss my beloved students, who have meaning for me as they explore their world. But here goes your thought gently bypassing my soul, forcing me to courageously look at my students, since to me they express the fear of dealing with the incompetence everyone who dares think of changing one's way in the world encounters."

"Maybe you'd end up loving the foreignness of the psychologist?"

Adam remained quiet at Guri's question, as if trying to absorb the meaning of the words 'love the foreignness'. Wasn't that a terminal illness all people flee? Was it possible to encounter oneself even more forcefully before a person who didn't even know your favorite cookie?

"Adam, are you with me? I hope I'm not stressing you with my caring," his friend asked.

"On the contrary, my dear friend! You don't know how positive your influence is on my world. I suddenly recalled our great love of planting new life stories for those strangers outside the café... why is such an activity so fond to our souls? Isn't it as wondrous as the opportunity to create a new world? A strange world for the reality of those people? Perhaps even I... perhaps even I can create some sort of a new reality within me, should I only let a strange person encounter me?"

Gentle smiles of honesty spread on their faces, accompanied by embarrassed laughs, like insight without the need for words. The silent monk occasionally relaxed his grip on the pillow and turned his gaze to both of them, while the furrows of his eyes creased as if feeling something.

These types of joyous sounds were uncommon to the ears of the doctor, since most of his work in that department made his beloved patients commit to the acceptable requirements of silence thanks to the latest state-of-the-art pills he'd give them. He found himself looking, trying to understand how these pills had such a different impact on each and every person, a kind of an alchemy of sensations.

Within all that, despite knowing that the use of medication was often considered salvation for some patients, he also realized that most of them had lost any chance of regaining a grip on their lives due to their dependency on said medications.

The doctor must've encountered his own conscience, without much choice, within an internal scream that faintly wondered if there was any point in refining his medical actions or whether it would merely be a façade, drawn from his inner need to feel like a person who mattered. His inner question often burned so hot he'd risked getting burned, and thus would immediately start obsessively going over the medical records of his many patients, detailed on sheets of paper so professionally tagged they seemed capable of describing more specifically inanimate objects than humans with beating hearts.

His increasing search made his bouncing eyes encounter that same secret destructive feeling hiding deep inside the soul of those who dared look at themselves from the outside, wondering whether he would've been proud of himself had he stepped aside and looked at himself. And from his honest reply, insulting his entity, his legs started to quickly move towards the mildest patients' rooms and discharge them, as a lifeline for his soul, from the suffocation of the killing insight.

"Hello, Adam, you… can be discharged right away. Here's your discharge letter, along with my single recommendation for you."

Adam and Guri looked at the doctor's face, embarrassed by their happiness as opposed to his relative unhappiness.

"That's it? So fast?" Adam asked, as if seeking to stay.

The doctor was desperate to protect his soul, and blurted out words rarely heard in those wards: "Yes, yes, you'll be fine, it's time you got back to your real life. Remember to give your soul space, consider it an act of grace."

Adam felt something concealed was taking place behind the scenes, but couldn't recognize what it was, and was even glad for the mystery of the tempest on the doctor's face as he left the room in haste, without even regarding the other patient, who – in turn – was left alone by everyone else. "Those in pain will forever find solace in the misery of others," Adam wondered to himself with a concealed smile as he put on his socks.

The silent monk went back to hugging his pillow, knowing that this experience was bound to end very soon.

The doctor continued to vigorously walk through the hospital hallways, as if fleeing a storm of complex emotions within himself. It sometimes seemed his feet were independent from the emotional processes within him, but deep down his inner storm had begun to slowly ebb, like the touch of a lake; he was aware that one good deed was able to cover many transgressions in his soul. There was amazement within him for he, as his beloved patients, was required to suppress his private horror by external means, so as not to implode into himself. His hidden thoughts would momentarily burst, as if willing to admit that his soul was flattered by his great status at the hospital; however, deep down he knew that the only difference between him and them was that they were able to express their terror without censoring themselves, as if still awaiting loved and containment, while he – and most people in the world – preferred to lie to themselves about it, reducing their feelings so long as they seemed to be holding on to guaranteed routes. These hidden words were tattooed on the back of his thoughts and helped him see the people in his care through kinder eyes, from a modesty of thought, since he knew he could also be one of them at any given moment.

He sometimes even wondered to himself where he'd gotten that moral stance, according to which he was so fair towards Adam and other patients he'd decided to discharge. And since the answer to this question was so clearly innate within him, he spent every moment reminding himself that the motivations leading him to become a doctor were nothing but an attempt to avoid the terrible helplessness he'd encountered as he saw his parents on their last journey as a child. The doctor knew in his heart, even without expressing it in words, that eventually all people drew themselves some sort of life story in an attempt to either get further from or closer to a meaningful traumatic memory they'd experienced, consciously or not.

These types of thoughts enfolded him like a close embrace, as if confessing his deepest emotions to an imaginary priest who wasn't there, such that cleansed his heart and allowed him to return to that same divine calling every morning.

3.

After taking off his hospital gown and putting on his clothes, Adam began to unwillingly think about the wretchedness of human life – those who might, in a split second, abandon the theater of roles in their world and find themselves in light and uniform clothing, without even noticing; cleansing from their flesh all the existential illusions they'd relied on and hung onto their entire lives. That hidden thought was severed, almost rescued, when the gaze of the silent man met his. It was clear his eyes expressed disappointment towards the loneliness that almost touched him, like a rejected child already anticipating what is to come, his entire existence expressing a mute scream.

Adam held onto the notion that he had to express his feelings to him, fearing he would soon leave this hospital and keep his loving words to himself, without sharing them, just as his loved ones had left him alone and full of doubt.

"Goodbye, unique man. Though I've never heard your voice, know that you have wordlessly spoken to my very soul.

You've served as an educator of simplicity to me, teaching me how beautiful the silence of observation is." After taking a few quick excited breaths, Adam knew there were a few more words he would like to express to him, out of the depths of his consciousness: "At first your strangeness only intensified my own, since I didn't know how one could willingly take on a life of muteness, but after a few hours I felt we were very close... we could have been best friends in another lifetime." Adam's words engulfed the man, who seemed to accept the love directed at him without fighting it off. The man continued his absent ways and lay his head on the pillow, as if seeking to give into sleep.

Adam looked at Guri and tried to find a comforting explanation that would set his mind at ease within all that helplessness. In their silence, the two expressed a consensus that what should've been said had already been said, and they could now go.

The two went out to the department's hallway with their feet striding at a significantly slow pace, as if obeying their uncontrollable curiosity to look at the facial features of the other patients who lay in strange poses on their beds. They certainly expressed their mental screams, unable to find peace.

Following many silent minutes, Adam could've looked into himself and imagined his own soul, which also sometimes found itself screaming to escape, in a rage that could not be concealed.

This sight made him wonder about the fate of people to his friend, out loud —

"Look at that... if they're so uncomfortable with themselves here, at the hospital, then life outside must be a hundred times more uncomfortable and difficult for them, right? Or perhaps I should think about it in a different way, that maybe those who suffer more here feel that way because the hospital prevents them from obsessively holding onto all those daily fabrications that help them reach the end of the day without noticing."

The sound of the words made Guri feel like his friend wished to express a power emerging out of him, like someone who'd already gotten over the hardships of the hospital. It was a kind of unaware attempt to make himself forget the memory of his fragility, which he knew could shatter at any given moment without him having any saying in the matter.

Guri remained silent in attentive sensitivity. Within him grew a thought complementing Adam's question, yet that was only common in his soul and not expressed in actual words until that very moment, and he said: "Life is hard for everyone, is it not? But there are only a few who dare admit it. Only a few of us can contain the fact of existence and live life as it really is, with courage and acceptance, without sweet comforts derived from the inability to submissively and humbly accept what everyone else is so vigorously hiding, you know… the bitter end in which they aren't taking part. That end which nulls all those long exertions, all those truly deep emotions."

Adam smiled at him with an appreciative tenderness for the space of thoughts they'd built between them through the years, a world in which no thought should be censored or concealed. His friend experienced goosebumps on his own flesh, this type of smiling gaze that could only exist between two people capable of imagining the possibility of non-existence.

He suddenly once again recalled that line from his journal and said it out loud: "It's dangerous to describe reality as it actually is."

"It certainly is, but in our space, there's no danger to be found," Guri replied.

~ ~ ~

The two left through the hospital gate, out into the multiple masses of the busy city which suddenly seemed like islands of loneliness within a raging ocean. In their silence, caressing thoughts started to form in their souls, as if they were wired to one another without admitting the emotional bridge between them. That profound love became a testament to why life was worth living, despite the daily hardships.

Adam suddenly stopped walking in abrupt distress, and from a bird's-eye view one could see a multitude of people passing him by in every direction. Guri shouted at him to keep walking, but it seemed that Adam couldn't hear him. Heartache stabbed at his being, perhaps from when he first felt the coping of the silent man who had nothing in the world but himself as he hugged his pillow. He suddenly felt, firsthand, that all those masses around him weren't necessarily different from that man, since most had no true friends with whom they could bare their naked souls; he therefore couldn't help but think that they found any kind of occupation to avoid encountering themselves alone.

This anxiety, occurring among that crowd of strangers, made him wonder if anyone in the world truly saw him, which made it clear he was loved and exposed before Guri and that love of his. "Only two people in a lifetime!" he shouted to himself in imaginative sounds. "I could only be myself, in all my soul's colors, before two people! What about the rest of the people? How are they holding onto lifetimes of loneliness? And what of that loved one of mine, did she feel herself prior to me? Where the hell is the cemetery in which our mental bridge – hers and mine – is buried?" he desperately asked.

Guri felt his friend drowning in his own deep end, choking, without any way to detach himself from his downward spiral. He therefore came running towards him, shaking his shoulders until he was fully awake. His opened eyes were brighter than ever, without having run red. In doing so, it seemed he was expressing a truth that was hard for himself to bear, with which he had made his peace.

"Are you alright? Stay with me, Adam."

"Yes, yes. These thoughts, they jump at me uncontrollably and are sometimes so sharp that the pain overwhelms me. But I remember that I'm allowed to surrender to moments in pain, everything eventually passes after all. I have to get some sleep, thank you for your existence, my dear friend. Thank you for being you… I should go back home and sleep now; I need to cease for a while. I need self-absence."

"Alright… write to me when everything dies down. Don't forget what the doctor recommended, and remember, I'm always here for you, whatever the circumstances."

~ ~ ~

Adam leaned on the kitchen counter, listening to the water boiling in the pot. He internally thought that his soul more closely resembled a volcano at constant war with the glaciers of his heart, and despite their infinite size they would humbly melt.

His recent anxiety was certainly a mirror of his defeat in life's theater… he was suddenly aware of himself and decided that he shouldn't commit to his thoughts, for they had neither end nor beginning, and it would be better for him to somewhat detach himself from his internal rummaging and step outside himself for a few moments.

He poured hot water into his teacup and turned to the living room, where he sat on the couch and closed his eyes for a few minutes to soak in the pleasant sensation of the lack of self. His lips blew at the water and his gaze started wandering between the house walls, as if trying to notice details anew: "Here's my journal… here's a little bush that got no attention for a while… here's a painting we once bought together, well… these are all objects. Objects painted with history. It seems nothing has changed in the house since she left… and perhaps she's here… perhaps she's here now more than ever before."

A frustrated look spread across his face, as if he were trying to shake and flee from the power of his thoughts that wouldn't let go.

"I have to separate from my past. I can't take it anymore; there's a hidden power within me forcing me to live in times that no longer exist, times where there's no way of knowing if they ever existed at all!

"Maybe I should listen to the doctor, and therapy will clarify some worlds for me?

"Maybe a forgetfulness pill has already been invented that can wipe out memories?

"A 24-hour pill, a week's worth of pills, a year's worth, many years' worth!

"They should receive a Nobel Prize for such medication!"

He suddenly listened to the unfiltered words spewing forth, and decided that had such a pill existed, he would never have been able to take it, as he knew in his very bones that most of his joy was concealed within the suffering of his memories.

In these dark moments he'd be reminded that he had to do whatever would help him stabilize his soul, from past experience, and immediately started writing lines in his journal, etching out the reality of the silent man's existence in his conscience, so he'd never forget him. He also certainly wanted to describe the final sense of rest he felt as he watched his many illusions detach him from conscious reality and into sweet and embracing worlds. He certainly wanted to remember Guri's loving friendship, who was present in his extreme moments of loneliness in the past. But before he started this Sisyphean labor of testimony, he turned to a random page in his journal so he could read an ancient testimony of his very own soul, in an attempt to prove the continuity of the timeline that was forever in doubt.

His eyes focused on a few sentences and his lips spoke the words inside his mind, until he suddenly started to repeat them aloud: "From the day I stood my ground, I've feared forgetfulness. When I loved, I could be separated from my mind, and in doing so forget my anxiety."

Adam bit his lips as the choked-up tears started to build inside him, until they were flowing out onto his cheeks and fingers, erasing his trembling feelings. He immediately wondered how it was possible that he was so relaxed in the sense of love, in distant times, that he valiantly pushed away his fight with existential anxiety, and wondered whether this was his own journal or a stranger's he had stumbled upon and adopted?

In those moments, his questions were greater than his capacity to contain them, and he felt himself in the silence of the deep end.

Acting yet unaware, Adam sipped from the boiling water that burnt his lips and his mouth, but at least it silenced his internal war for a few moments, with sharp urgency. A strange twitch started to evolve in his face, as if he suddenly understood how one could rise above mental suffering. He gently discovered all those many people in the hospital, who found themselves there after having hurt themselves in various ways. Adam decided these were only temporary solutions to human existence, which served as a constant terror for some people.

He knew his soul was far from such violent solutions, but couldn't hold onto a deep inner conviction. He wondered whether his obsessive thoughts regarding nonexistent times weren't considered in examining even more hurtful behavior, and therefore began thinking of all those moments in the world when his soul was at ease, in an enveloping peace, where he experienced himself in the best way.

"I know there are quite a few moments like these. I know. I just… I just sometimes have a hard time recalling them when I'm reoccupied with doubts about myself, but there are doubtless quite a few moments like that. I have to remember what's really important, what gives me vitality," he said to himself while sipping the tea that had lost its destructive power and become pleasant. "As if every choice I make determines my world. Every single choice changes something. I wake up different every day. But in the end… in the end, I have to remember the humblest reason that makes life worth living. I must not forget it. Even if events overwhelm me and lead me to anxiety… I have to remember the smallest smile… the most hidden thought… the first caress. I have to learn how to tattoo the ability to experience the range of my emotions on my soul, without violent judgment of my humanity."

A chill spread through Adam's body as he heard his latest words. He quickly wrote them down on his testimonial pages. He suddenly wondered what the difference was between the inner thoughts he heard in his soul, and the thoughts expressed in actual speech. Was that the reason he had been offered therapy? Where he could speak out on himself without any censorship, like the prayer of a man who could say words that did not exist in any other language?

Tender excitement built up in his stomach and he began thinking how he might find a psychologist for his own soul; how did one know who best to become emotionally naked with? After all, it wasn't a long-term friendship in which both would gradually add up gentle layers of loving and secure senses, allowing the courageous expression of soul secrets. Nor was it a known love story between two people who would allow themselves to bare both body and soul.

"Isn't it a terrible bet to strip down in your thoughts, to be so naked, so exposed... without having any good eyes? Isn't it better then to stay in the familiar world, the hidden rooms of my soul?" he asked himself out loud.

These kinds of defensive questions met him like internal doubts, screaming at him with desperation and sophistication. It seems they'd hidden inside of him like leeches, waiting many years until they were able to burst out with their words, deeply convincing him to keep devoting himself to the familiar paths, and God forbid not experience anything new that might be good for him.

The reddening face of his student suddenly came up in his imagination, and he began comparing his own fears to her innocent world. *I recall the jittering of her eyes and her trembling voice in those moments. How did she dare express herself so bravely? Where did such a young girl gain the ability to be so much herself?* he excitedly thought. Within this he wished to plant in his heart the thought that he also had within him that capability for inner exposure.

Adam began smiling to himself as someone who understood, perhaps for the first time, his envy of the innocence of his students, who had so many opportunities to ask unasked questions at such young ages. Maybe he fantasized about going to treatment, where he could say anything that came to mind like a small child beholden to no one. It was a longing for others to accept and marvel at and thrill at his words, a bit like a mother accommodating everything the child would bring.

Then his inner voice arose: *Before my family, my best friends, the love of my life… I've always been a version of myself, a changing range of colors, a kind of changing viewpoint… even though I've been stripped down to a blunt soulful nudity… perhaps since it's a strange encounter, my soul will allow itself to go beyond itself… maybe I'll be able to express words never before heard? Maybe I'll be able to express hidden thoughts that are forbidden, or maybe even illegal to express? Maybe I'll find soulful colors within me that have never been seen.*

~ ~ ~

Adam touched his lips, which still ached from the last sip, and his fingers inadvertently turned to caress the hairs on his head, like someone observing his final thoughts and trying to understand the meanings deriving from them.

He suddenly stood up and took the teacup, to wash it and the accumulated dishes. A mosquito clung to one of the sink's walls and seemed to gallantly fight for its continued existence, as its legs flailed about, asking to be rescued. But Adam washed it down to its death, like a guiltless child's game.

That was how Adam found himself severely giving in to cleaning the house. His hand held on to the rag and he started wiping stains off the kitchen floor. The more his arms sweat in effort, the more he was able to bear himself. The more he insisted on making his search for hidden dirt more stern and extreme, the more powerful and confident he felt, since he destroyed them quickly and successfully, as opposed to his mental searches.

As he looked on what was happening under his bed for the first time, his head went red, his veins stuck out as if seeking to burst, and a strange and absurd smile slightly spread on his lips.

While acting, he talked to himself out loud and said: "It makes me so happy that there are other solutions to get away from myself rather than hurting my lips. I'll simply fill my time with non-stop activities, as like a factory worker unable to stop and observe, he had no option to remove himself from the binding demands. I'll clean the house every day, sweep every corner, make a shopping list, plan tomorrow's lesson, throw out the garbage, tremble with self-pleasure and go to sleep. One can certainly go through an entire lifetime this way. That's how all people operate nowadays, hiding without admitting it."

Adam smiled to himself. At the same time, he tied the garbage bag shut and went out to throw it into the large trash bin up the street. How nice it must be for all the neighbors to throw their garbage into another bin, further away from their homes. How nice it must be to have someone else deal with the horrible smell. How nice it must be not having to deal with their garbage by themselves in their homes. Everyone needed to have a larger trash bin outside their home.

Everyone needed to free the leftovers of their souls. *I need to be emptied. I realize that now. What a genius invention! A garbage truck for the soul, that empties at a certified landfill once a week, without guilt, without sanitation fines…*

4.

These thoughts from yesterday remained etched in Adam's consciousness as he was on his way to the bus stop. With his persistent steps, he paid excess notice to the trash cans around him. It now seemed that their meaning had changed for him, having realized it wasn't just his basic need to clear himself of the dirt that had clung to him during his lifetime, but also his compulsive need to know there were trashcans that smelled even worse than his. There was comfort in dealing with that.

Adam suddenly sniffed and probed the various cans like a dog, greatly attesting to the height of others struggling around it. One thing was certain – there was no trashcan around that didn't smell like terror.

As his feet led him to the bus stop, so did his curiosity grow regarding whether he'd meet the old man who had so bluntly dismissed his existence. His anxiety was now lessened after thinking about that man's trashcans, where he had surely been thrown into extreme struggle many times, as if it were unsurprising and even acceptable that he was better off not remembering anything.

It's one thing for the old man to have vicariously accepted his fate, since he resolved the terror of life by completely forgetting it – what will happen to my own world? After all, most of my existence is just an attempt to try and minimize myself down to my lost memories in the deep lakes, serving as proof that I still deserve to live. How great is the absurdity I carry within me that I constantly doubt my memories, since my soul is attacking itself both from the front and from behind, with decisive and merciless sophistication.

While speaking to himself, he suddenly realized that it had been many days since he was able to so clearly articulate these sensations, even though he'd felt his anxiety in his bones for many years, as an internal hidden creation one could touch but never see.

How nice it would be for him to hold onto the exposure of the fields of his soul, if even for a moment, as though it were a picture full of bright colors, even if he clearly and specially captured but one black speck of existence, just to see it in its entire glory, without masks, without concealing fabrications. The intensity of the experience was further validated as he was able to get closer to himself and understand his utmost existential anxiety by encountering the misery of the other, of all things.

The two stood next to each other in complete silence, as though they'd never met before. Their gazes crossed by chance, without any twinge of memory.

The old man's demeanor projected an existential serenity that didn't try and hide any guilty secret regarding past events.

Adam looked at the old man's calm breaths, and felt in his bones the great cost of being a man aware of his internal wars, compared to the lightness of the man who sophisticatedly removed the bold colors of existence from himself.

A gentle jealousy grew in his soul. He too wanted to experience the gentle breaths of serenity.

Just like that, without paying attention, out of eternal recurrence, Adam found himself inside images of early life, looking at the old man talking to the bus driver while sitting in that same back seat.

"I look at reality as I picture it in my familiar consciousness; these are my eyes looking at old memories, these are my hands holding onto that same rigid banister, and still… how is it that I'm unable to recognize who I was before my latest anxiety? It feels strange and alienating to be so different from myself, each time anew," he quietly said to himself, for fear he might be discovered.

~ ~ ~

Adam got off at the bus stop and slowly approached the school gate, where he met many familiar looks that effortlessly projected caressing thoughts onto him, warming his very soul. "Where there's love, existential foreignness loses its power," the thought came into his mind with a gentle smile, accentuating how fragile he'd been before life's events uncontrollably plagued him.

A chill went down his back, his longing for his class surfaced at once and a burst of excitement surged through him.

"Hello everyone, I'm sorry I've been missing class. Even teachers need sick days sometimes," he excitedly said to his students.

The students smiled at each other in silence.

"Before we start, I'd like to ask you all how you felt at the end of our last class. After all, we agreed that everyone's alone in their feelings, and that can be very lonely to contain."

The students shifted uncomfortably.

A slender hand was raised, and Adam moved left, towards it, and said: "Yes, please."

The boy's sunken eyes seemed to have burrowed inside him as a hiding spot. His eyes suddenly stuck out like a bursting expression of thought.

The boy moved his gaze away and said: "I wanted to thank you, the one over by the window! You, whose voice I've never heard in class before. I wanted to thank you for being the first one to admit to loneliness. I wanted to thank you for being brave and shyly shouting out what everyone's been feeling, what everyone's been afraid of. Maybe now... maybe when everyone's lonely but brave to admit it, we're a bit less lonely. Because we don't have to hide as much, fake it as much; it's more present, here, in class, in our gazes. I'm glad I don't have to lie as much. I'm glad other people have it rough, like, I'm not glad you have it rough but I'm glad I'm not alone in it. That my experience doesn't put me as far on the outside as I previously thought."

The girl's eyes reddened from those direct words, strengthening her spirit.

"More hands for sharing any thoughts?" Adam asked.

"Ahh!" the boy kept going. "This means we're not the only ones feeling lonely, but also our parents, grandparents, the celebrities on TV, and also… hmmm… you too."

The students didn't know what to think, since his words overstepped any acceptable boundaries of conversation. Some of them even secretly laughed, as if encountering hidden gossip full of meaning.

Adam suddenly found himself in emotional turmoil, like vomit forever present in the walls of his stomach for exact moments of existential nausea, saving him from what he couldn't bear.

Seconds passed without presence, like someone absent from reality seeking to flee as an act of survival, without the ability to put it into words.

Within him he thought that all of his anxiety was now exposed for his students to see, as if they could see even his deepest yearnings to detach from himself, so as to not allow the boy to inscribe embarrassment on his soul.

In search of self-relaxation, he met the kind eyes of the girl, and she sent him a thousand soundless positive words. He once again recalled how he'd held her feelings in the earlier encounter, and how he was now lost inside of his.

Adam found himself leaning tightly on the table, holding onto it as a stable source to regain his composure and return to reality, to all those eyes awaiting his response.

His thoughts started acting within him, as if wishing to reply to the boy with some words, not as a desperate move on a chessboard but first in thought, and then in honesty that would set an example for all those struggling with their souls.

His eyes turned to the embarrassed boy.

Adam stood up straight, brought his hands to his chest and said: "Right. What you say is true. I too experience loneliness. In fact, I've been experiencing it more than ever at this time in my life..."

A silence full of internal conversation filled the classroom. Embarrassment started spreading among those present.

The boy suddenly rose to his feet and asked: "And what do you do with this loneliness? It isn't nice at all, it's quite unbearable, it's really awful!"

Sounds were heard around the classroom, as if they were angry at the insolence of his insensitive questions, penetrating and improper... even though the mere fact of articulating the question and the courage to express every thought fascinated everyone.

Adam gently smiled. He was glad for the question, which he intended to answer quite successfully. He knew the very depths of his fragile soul, and thus also the burning sense he had that no one in this world was impervious to the hardships of human loneliness.

"I'm not sure you're going to like my answer. I don't like my answer so much myself, but I've learned firsthand that it's not a good question."

"Why is it not a good question? It's an excellent question!" the boy replied.

"It's an inappropriate question because it contains a hidden premise, a wish, claiming in the darkness that life was meant to be good. Not just good, but constantly pleasant. However, reality confronts us with such a wide range of emotions – like an endless rainbow – from the greatest happiness to indescribable terror. Within all of these, you and I also encounter loneliness. What can you do with it? Nothing but live with it, allow it to be, exist with it, accept it and its existence, and accept the experience of life as it is, despite what it is," Adam said with a measure of fright; perhaps he had overstepped his responsibility in educating his students.

"It really is an annoying answer! Maybe you're saying these things because you're not as young as we are. Maybe your colors aren't as smiling and bright as they used to be. Maybe you're to blame for everything you feel," the boy yelled at him, having seemingly lost his composure.

Adam could contain the boy's turmoil, and after the latter had sat down and gently breathed in, he slowly approached, close enough to touch his shoulder and say: "You're right, my answer really is annoying. But it's trying to remain honest and humble in thought. It helps me shake the unreasonable bar of expectations within our souls, insisting on deciding life is one great joy without any evidence. After all, you've seen for yourself how you reveled in the words of your classmate regarding loneliness. You saw how her feelings seemed to be planted within you, within me and everyone else. Why do we have to hide from each other in wishes that are unattainable anyway? You understand, dear student? I don't do anything in the face of loneliness, I don't fight it, because my heroism will be holding onto this contradiction and even relishing it, because I'm an active participant in the world. I accept the rules of the game even though I don't like them all," he summed up, with words that touched the young hearts.

The bell rang and the students quickly went out to the yard.

The boy's sensations became more complicated, as he passed by Adam and whispered: "I don't like all the rules either."

~ ~ ~

Adam went down the stairs and sat on a bench in the yard. He looked at the young kids playing ball, his eyes relentlessly dancing from one side to the other, following the ball that knew to take pleasure in individuals while mainly evading most players...

They're chasing conquests, uncertain whether they'll attain them or not. They believe, beyond all reason, that it's worth fighting for. It's worth sacrificing for; they hold so much passion! One can almost imagine they don't care about the end. Yearning is the matter itself, the catharsis, pure, innocent and addictive tension that stays in their consciousness that has yet to look high above. The curiosity present in a soul that knows how to appreciate the earthly, he thought to himself in an internal attempt at admonishment.

A gentle voice addressed him; he didn't hear it. The attention of his spirit was at one with the young warriors on the field, who to him expressed his jealousy of them, since they were able to become addicted to the present, without escaping to faraway wars of the soul that had no known cure.

"Adam!" the girl once again called out to him, in an overly loud voice. He turned his gaze to her and asked how she was doing, and the former sat next to him. "He was over the line, wasn't he? You shouldn't ask such questions so bluntly, without any consideration, lacking politeness."

"You shouldn't be mad at him. He was simply experiencing a pure moment of existence in which he acknowledged something hidden within the soul, but unlike the norm, he was also able to articulate it in words, painting or touch." He looked into her eyes and kept going. "You should be proud of yourself; he'll never forget you."

"Thank you, Adam, I hope there are better days ahead of you. It isn't easy knowing you're also in pain sometimes. While it's brave that you've exposed yourself to us that way, it's uneasy for us to know it. We young people need someone to look up to," she said with innocent honesty.

"I see where you're coming from, but I couldn't do anything other than tell the truth. Looking ahead, it'll be better for everyone."

The girl accepted his words and went on her way. Adam watched her image walking away, and a large smile spread across his soul. He appreciated her empathy for people, especially since she was shy. In that way she resembled and reminded him of his younger self, when he knew how to give in to entire worlds of creation without having to utter every word.

Joyful shouts were heard from the field. A group of young boys stood together in a victorious hug. Their apparent desire hypnotized Adam into a being of nail-biting curiosity regarding the battle that had just been determined.

How beautiful their excitement is, how beautiful it is for them to sweat in such a positive way. They're happy, purely by the cooperation that's so irregular in this universe. They're happy because they managed to overcome an external challenge together. They're certainly nothing like me. They're not happy with the wrenched sense of the loser. They're happy at having outdone themselves and not because of the other's inferiority, he thought.

He suddenly looked inward once again, and recalled the boy who had accused him of loneliness. *Maybe I should presently look at life's events with a criticizing view into mine? I certainly don't belong to those who outdo themselves; on the contrary, my soul embraces inferiority. My soul dwells in the cellars of longing for my old love. My soul is obsessed with doubts in the face of times that no longer exist. My defeat has become a house of meaning on which existential anxiety is painted in endless shades. It suddenly seems to me that I've turned sadness into a masterpiece that only I witness. Is this melancholy not but narcissism pulsating within me out of self-wallowing that knows no bounds?* he asked the jury of his soul's trial.

Adam went on thinking: *Had the sad people of this world heard my words, they'd become violent to this criticism. These find love and gratification in the war of self-disgust, as if it were the solution to their gnawing loneliness. How rude! The contempt! How can one doubt the deep sadness of people, as if they'd chosen it in their souls, in a hidden joy to which they could not yet admit?*

I have to silence these thoughts. I've spent many years of my life scratching my emotional wounds; how could I otherwise commit, without some kind of hidden pleasure I'm not yet ready to admit to? Should I confess that my grasp on the pain is a testament to me being a struggling person in the world?

One thing's crystal clear to me: a person's most impressive ability is to suffer. Anyone can be a prodigy. A prodigy of inferiority.

How much joy must human beings make of their ability to live as they are, despite life? It's probably the most common sport in the world. If the students only knew how great my skills are in this field…

5.

As night fell, small streetlamps lit up on the main boulevard where Adam walked all alone. His sight was drawn to the many leaves gathering on the sidewalk.

A gentle smile spread across his face as he was able to momentarily detach himself from his winding consciousness and give in to simple existence with a magical sense of addiction. But immediately – as if in a violent upheaval – he realized within his spirit that it was a tiny moment of joy, a gentle moment of existence in which he was one with that thing, without longing, without any desire, only an innocent devotion to existence.

Ah! I too can enjoy a moment of happiness! he thought; how unkind life was in this matter. There were many joyful moments, mostly joy in superiority over others, or at least stemming from the shortcomings of others. *However, clean moments of joy are an uncommon elation, since they're impartial, exposed only to those capable of appreciating that which is most humble*, he said to himself excitedly. While doing so, he understood that a great illness had spread in his soul, causing him to dig through his thoughts about life, often without really experiencing them. *Here's a magical moment of life in which I've touched the light! Though the light faded as soon as I was aware of it.*

Thus, Adam found himself looking into the eyes of the people walking past him, like a man desperately looking for the familiar gaze of his old love. So many eyes looked back at him, yet there wasn't a single real encounter. A transparent sense of existence started to spread within him, such that could drown any gentle soul.

Maybe they're like me, searching for old soulmates through the city streets. Maybe they also lost all their memories and are looking for pieces of information about the lake of longing, to which they have no access. Had I only been able to stop living that which died, died like nothing could ever die again... no matter, every person needs some memories of life, thanks to which they can tell themselves that not all their efforts were in vain, he thought to himself while his gaze was drawn to a dirty street-dweller wearing layers of colorful coats. The man's eyes were fragile and gentle, and there was much joy emerging from them, since he was able to expose himself in bright colors and dance his soul away in free movements, as if he was alone in the world.

He's more colorful and stands out more than everyone else! Maybe he's also desperate for a mother's gentle caress? Maybe he's also wishing to be found...

This internal wondering gave Adam chills. He thought about his recent life events, in which he met people who taught him about fragile human existence while most of the teaching was done in complete silent observation of their gentle faces.

The old man remembers no one. The silent man hugging the pillow... and that discarded person performing a dance without an audience.

Winds of anxiety raged on the cusp of his consciousness; tiny fiery sparks desperate for a gust of wind so they could become a violent inferno. But this time it seemed that his anxiety failed, and stronger forces within his soul overcame it and fled the fear that he would someday end up as one of them.

Before his eyes he saw the image of a man standing on the edge of a cliff, his neck stretched towards the abyss with peak curiosity, then immediately returning to himself for fear of survival, to avoid being nullified forever. All it would take was a slightly stronger gust of wind and he would fall.

After escaping the horror, Adam began envying the souls of the old man, the silent man and the discarded one. With inexplicable sophistication they'd escaped their basic dependency on others, as if freeing themselves from the invisible bonds that had taken hold of his hands and threatened his existence and choices with heavy metal chains. Did he find their existence alluring? They had become transparent people, without a memory lake into which he was sucked against his will, without understanding why or having the ability to be rescued.

His envious look sought to further his investigation and determine what these people gained from their choice to live on the road of loneliness. Unlike his conversation with his students, where they had humbly determined loneliness to be a part of life, this was a mental decision to permanently isolate themselves from others until they became invisible, colorless. They actually held on to the possibility of being "nothing" within life itself, as if they'd heard his conversations with Guri when they'd brought up the possibility that they might never have been born, and no one would have noticed their absence. But compared to them, they actually exercised that thought while still alive. They were gone… utterly gone, yet in some utterly unthinkable way they might have been holding onto life more than ever.

How was it possible to exist this way for an entire lifetime? In shame he started to wonder deep down why they didn't annul their existence, whether their freedom was but proof of the power of life overcoming every terror.

What was it in their routine that gave them the power to be alive?

There has to be something! A hidden secret, some despicable transcendence. Such diabolical capability to show us... they must certainly enjoy the doubt and anxiety developing within our souls that one day we'll become like them, and maybe even take it further! Perhaps the most hidden joy is in their knowledge that we are incapable of bearing their world, and that only they have reached such a transcendent level – that hard-to-find mental elevation – by carrying indescribable human suffering.

After leaving the street-dweller and finally reaching the essence of his knowledge on the matter, Adam began to turn on the boulevard, though he didn't know where his feet were taking him. It was clear to him just how common loneliness was.

He immediately responded to himself: *All the people in my life are like computers filled with data of terror and joy... parameters of passions, wants, traumas and smiles, you don't know just how believable they are, or perhaps they're hiding mental covers and debts... but what am I? Where am I in all of this? What is it within me that preserves this yearning to dive into the basement of my memories, my old love, the person I was? What draws me to the dark, deep end where there is nothing but deadly suffocation? What's so pleasurable about my own doom? It's certainly not in vain.*

~ ~ ~

Many hours of wandering went by without delay. The streets emptied, and it seemed that Adam was seeking to tire himself out until he couldn't help but fall asleep and suspend his soul in some form other than suffering. What mattered was to stop thinking, stop asking, stop observing life's events.

Desperation brought him to an internal agreement that he could sleep in the park tonight. But the possible offense suddenly rose in him, and from it he drew the power to quickly flee to his house. A familiar smile spread on his face, like someone able to laugh at himself for a moment after finding fiery strengths in favor of life within, of all things, the deep threatening his existence.

As he arrived home, he immediately stripped down and went to take a hot shower, which positively narrowed his being into his body, while closing his eyes and having no invasive thoughts.

Adam fell asleep at once, as if overcoming himself with rural tricks. But his soul – unbounded to his affairs – painted him an imaginative dream in which he was in an old bookstore, holding a used copy of *Notes from the Underground*[1], containing mental testimonies written in pencil on the margins of the pages as final thoughts, the notes of a reader skilled in the abyss...

He immediately started wondering if he'd be able to erase the last remainders of that man's soul, and whether that was nothing more than an intentional killing.

His objection to the act was honest, yet forces stronger than him compelled him to buy the book in order to confront the finite act that would be carried out upon someone without their knowledge. Within that, he found himself holding onto the pages, looking at the first note that linked the written words to *White Nights*[2], which he knew. Two of his fingers held onto an eraser, and internal excitement began to build

---

[1] Dostoevsky
[2] ibid

inside him as he wondered what would be the meaning of erasing one random word within an entire note. *One missing word and a person's entire intent can drastically change. It's so easy to be misunderstood, lost, disappearing… so many life notes I'm able to dismiss here, as if they never existed… but how can I do that? Maybe they also feared being forgotten so they wrote down intimate thoughts, a testament to their soul? And maybe they wished their loved ones would read their books after they were gone, as an inheritance of thoughts? Oh my, how can I perform an act of killing the soul of a stranger? Still, something about it is inviting… their notes are fascinating to me, but above all I must know how I'd feel to erase their words and not remember what they'd written… as if I've decided it'll disappear away into the deep lakes of forgetfulness… just as that loved one of mine was lost*, he thought.

It seemed his soul was secretly confronting him in the depths of the dream with the terror that he couldn't bear actual life, and this pronounced itself before him until he couldn't detach himself from the panic. *One word. Maybe I'll just erase one word? Here, she's already gone. She's gone but I still remember her, but in a few minutes I'll be occupied with my routine affairs and then that word will be my own private murder victim. Maybe I'll claim I can remember her in the context of the other words! So it would be better to erase the entire note, why should I pain myself with longing? All the words evaporate… I've forcefully erased all the words. Now I'll certainly get to hold onto total forgetfulness. I'll kill some certainty now, putting to death a person who's been long-dead. Nothing else could be more dead.*

Adam writhed in bed. Cold sweat spread through his body as his consciousness returned to full awakening. He knew from experience that his soul was sensitively stretching itself towards his deep fears, but was inexplicably also capable of stopping itself, invoking the needs of his body as he got up to use the bathroom.

Fragments from his latest dream still remained clear to him, and he immediately started writing them down. He had to tell Guri about the dream.

Do people spend their whole lives chasing the most distilled testament of their souls with the excuse of loving another, thanks to which they're only capable of getting closer to themselves? he thought to himself while writing down the dream. *The beloved other carries an exceptional soul-testament of themselves and they're lost within it, since it's capable of looking into the depths of their lost soul.*

What would I do if Guri disappeared as part of life's events? Who would I be without him carrying my soul's testament around the world? How would I be able to bear my own soul's testament with such loneliness… so much of me would be swallowed by the darkness as he left!

Maybe I can now understand the choices of those strange people who found solutions to loneliness. They knew how rare the ability is to truly strip down our soul with another. They knew they were incapable of it, and therefore allowed themselves to embrace private loss within familiar pains, if only to no longer deal with that hidden wish…

Nonstop thoughts of this sort were often experienced as storms entering from the outside, churning his guts and leaving him helpless.

Adam quickly got up to wash his face in cold water, to actualize his being back in freezing reality and ease his escape from his internal thoughts. Gentle and soft colors were reflected in his eyes, in the mirror he gazed into. During this process he was filled with wonder, how magical they were and the extent to which he'd been unable to see them for such long periods of time, when he was busy with the sad tunes of existence – and there was much beauty present in him now as well.

He suddenly noticed the gentle wrinkles painted around his bright eyes, signs of fatigue attesting to the intensity of his affairs. His eyes seemed to roll back, busy with insatiable and obsessive internal rummaging.

The ringing of his phone abruptly interrupted Adam's string of self-reflective thoughts. Guri's name appeared on the screen and an enveloping calm started spreading through him.

"Guri… you have no idea how much I need your presence right now."

"How are you? How are your days looking?"

"You know, same old turmoil. The pain is present as it has always been, and I can't make sense of it. The punctures of existence change in rhythm but are still present; you know, Guri, you certainly understand…"

"Can you share more with me, Adam? Explain it further to me."

"I've been wandering lately, trying to understand myself. Your words about me holding onto the dead past penetrated my being with such force that I couldn't contain them anymore; despite that, I thank you for being able to express what you meant to me."

"I couldn't do it any other way… that's our way of looking at life as it really is."

"I know, it's just… life's been too turbulent lately, and it seems I'm trying to hold onto something firm. And you know, my thoughts are sometimes an island of stability, but sometimes they fluctuate… these leaps between the wonderful and the dreadful. I have to share with you with some excitement that I was able to express the range of my emotions in the world around you, since you carry my exceptional soul's testament within you, what I couldn't express to anyone else in the world… not even to that loved one of mine… and as excited as I am by my thought, I'm also filled with fear of what I'd do if you were no longer in the world and I'd be on this life's journey by myself. I suddenly realize that everything has to be forgotten, and disappear as if it never existed…"

"Adam, my friend, we're too modest to judge life from the position of its finality. It's not really important that our being won't leave a mark. The only thing that's important is your existence and mine, even in these very moments in which we're able to express extreme thoughts and emotions. How did you put it? An exceptional soul's testament. These words have hardly been uttered since the Book of Chronicles! We must decisively hold onto the knowledge that we've succeeded at the highest task in the universe, even though it isn't written anywhere. We were a small light of existence, a beautiful light of honesty. Clear moments of humanity, a wide range of emotions. And so even though each moment brings us even closer to definite finality, we'll be ready to stand tall and express to ourselves that we accept life as it is, and despite what it is." Guri went silent for a moment, then added: "Are my words too long? Did you understand what I said?"

"You gave me chills," Adam said in tears. "To accept life as it is, despite what it is..."

"It's not like we have any other choice! After all, we – like everyone else – grew up into a distorted view of existence, the illusion that we can avoid the sicknesses of existence, the unbearable terror... but unsurprisingly we've also encountered extreme experiences, such that destroy common illusions and thus also destroy the greatest of comforts: the illusion that you can adopt other illusions. All that's left for us to do is bravely look at life as it is. Take part in existence, despite its sometime-embodiment of true terror as it probably appears to you in the terror of complete forgetfulness."

"Yes, it's quite unforgettable! It pierces my bones and even my dreams. Just yesterday I saw myself in the illusion of sleep, holding onto a book with notes written on the margins of its pages, and my desire to erase them was uncontrollable, since I at first projected my biggest fear onto another person in the world, and finally expressed a real ability in the face of the helplessness I know so well. And you know… the more I erased their words, the more my disappointment grew and my anxiety increased, as I learned how to uncover the mental dynamics that pulsate within me and perhaps even within other souls around the world. This yearning to make it through the greatest difficulty in our souls unscathed, in a range of versatile ways… only to eventually find out there's no magical path to be cleansed of the pains of existence. I'd have to make my peace with my share, my private suffering. After all, there's no other life waiting for me… no other life for anyone but that in which we found ourselves, without having chosen it. So all I've left to do is create myself, despite the constant grief in my soul," he quietly said, also concealing some excitement.

"Adam, I wish it were that simple... I can honestly tell you that only very few of us are capable of pushing their soul's energy into a position in life where they'd agree to experience the entire range of emotions, yet also accept the terror of life – without the common pattern in which they have to deny and clothe reality with various illusions! We'd have to pay heavy prices for the sake of moving towards a humble living position of this kind. We'd have to admit we've lost many years of existence while being strangers to ourselves, so distant...

It's inconceivable that we should attach this to ourselves, one might think it's not even worth acknowledging. The regression now bursts at such a high volume that the crack becomes infinite, despair becomes present. Maybe that's also why you, my soulmate, encounter your anxiety so strongly during this period in your life."

Adam's eyes welled up. He found his friend's words hiding deep inside him. "You know, I can certainly express with you what the doctor asked me to search for with the psychologist. But I suddenly find myself reminded of my complex conversations with my students, and I already told myself back then that these kinds of life lessons have to come in small dosages so we could contain them. After all, isn't that what the doctor ordered for me? To slowly express my deepest thoughts, to encounter my most nucleic figure with my voice and be closer to it, slowly, without any sin of censoring shame, just like those small doses of education that one can live with?"

6.

Pleasant sensations of relaxation took root in Adam for many days after he was able to extraordinarily and bravely express words that had been censored and hidden even from him. His anxiety, as he knew from experience, was expressed at the highest level since it created an unbridgeable gap between his known image and the emotional pain that erupted, perhaps from the difficulty of finding human words to describe his emotional turmoil. His stride in the world now became lighter, as if he'd unchained himself from the shackles of existence he'd unknowingly carried with him for so many years. How exciting it was to finally see his suffering in his eyes as a tangible and living thing, after having had it tattooed beneath his skin for so long.

"I managed to voice emotions and words that were not only clear to me firsthand, but were such that even Guri could find himself in my pain, thus being able to see myself more pronouncedly," he excitedly said to himself as he left his home.

He looked for the old man at the bus stop, his eyes darting, and it seemed his absence stood out more than anything. "Where could he be? Has he changed his ways and habits, or did he drown in that damned human lake of forgetfulness, finally vanishing into utter nonexistence?" he asked within himself.

Adam got on the bus and moved towards that familiar back seat. The quiet drive slightly resembled those same gentle moments of the absence of self and the caressing comfort he'd encountered in his hospital bed. An embracing cradle, free of invasive thoughts.

His eyes turned to the mirror above the driver's head. He wanted to understand the driver's mood through his reflection, which seemed unconcerned for the old man, as if secretly admitting relief that his help wasn't needed anymore. The driver's hands firmly held onto the steering wheel as a sound source of life he led and directed on his way. It sometimes seemed he was even better at his job when directing his attention to the news on the radio, which endlessly described the suffering of the masses in various topics. He sometimes had a hidden feeling of some unconscious inner happiness, joyful for everything stable in his life compared to the hardships of the people around him. His soul seemed to secretly beg for eternal, violent distractions that would put him as far away from himself as possible.

Adam was envious of him for being able to shake the burden of thought.

He got off the bus and turned onto the main path. He noticed from afar his beloved student sitting on the lawn, her legs crossed, eyes turned to the boy sitting in front of her, the same boy who had overwhelmed him with his loneliness.

A gentle excitement spread through his body. *These two must certainly find hidden thoughts in their souls right now, such that turn their eyes into fields of love accompanied by an embarrassment one can do nothing but give in to.* The closer he got to them, the more he feared that his presence might interrupt them, since he knew how rare that sensation was between people.

Had she not expressed herself in class, she probably would've been lost in her internal world, in terrible loneliness... and miraculously, out of her own exposure, the boy had also dared strip down in his thoughts. *Words can cause so much movement in a person*, he thought to himself. Tremors of consciousness gripped him for a moment, until sounds from the deep submissively erupted within him – *it's dangerous to describe life as it is, it's dangerous to describe life as it is...*

Adam breathed his familiar thoughts into gentle moments, until he looked at the delicate space of the two once more and concluded: *Maybe it's just dangerous to look at life as it is without the ability to describe it as it is, at least for one person in the world who understands you.*

Adam opened the classroom door, and the students took their seats and looked at his face, curious to encounter that space of exploration they found so intriguing once again. The absence of the couple evoked a fear in their minds that maybe they'd given up on the option of examining their thoughts further in class, but Adam knew the two had forgotten themselves on the school's lawn due to their gentle excitement from their encounter, which made the reality of time redundant.

"What would you like to talk about today? Or to be exact, what question would you have us look at from different angles?" he turned to his students.

One of the students asked to speak, and Adam turned his attention to him.

"The last time my classmates spoke in class, I realized I'm alone in the world and no one can really know me and get close to who I really am. I wanted you to know it was very hard for me to hear and see just how much I can't resist it. It was a painful internal terror for me, and when I got home at the end of that day, I went straight to bed, because I didn't want to think about it anymore. But when I woke up to my parents fighting, I asked myself how much we actually dare to tell people who we really are, what we really feel. Maybe this loneliness is actually a side-effect because we're afraid to talk to each other and honestly expose ourselves, and not, as you said, because it's an inseparable part of life?" he asked in a gentle voice.

An elevated heartbeat spread through Adam's unfamiliar body parts, his eyes smiled with excitement for the innocence of his student's loving thought, which made one of his very own fears ever so present.

"Your words take us one step further in our joint investigation, and dare I rephrase, I'd have to ask this class two questions: is this experience really shared by all of us? Are we all hiding within our souls and only exposing very little of them to the people around us?"

Adam's questions, etched deep within his soul, now met the gentle eyes of his students. They found themselves within his words, unable to hide.

The students' silence intensified the overall embarrass-ment that spread through the classroom. They had to avert their eyes from that exposed encounter with their peers.

The classroom door squeaked and opened wide, making it easier on them to escape themselves for a while as the pair apologized for being late and made their way to their seats.

"Good to have you back," Adam said to them, happy to emphasize the students' curiosity regarding those who dared undress their souls in public. "We were just finding out today how much we allow ourselves – if at all – to express our darkest thoughts in exposed honesty to other people in the world, or at least one person in the world."

The two met each other's gaze as they heard Adam's words.

Adam walked around his table and scanned the classroom. He was aware that the silent tune, momentarily present in the shared space, now addressed a pure inner truth within their souls, and any word spoken would sabotage the experience.

After a few moments of staring, the nullifying silence intensified an unclear internal anger within the girl, so much so that her eyes began to turn red. She raised her hand at once. Her voice trembled, as if hesitating, and it seemed that her words had to be shouted out: "No one teaches us that we can and should really express ourselves. We're always being asked to be good. Good to who? You grownups. And what were you thinking? You're the ones to really blame for all this loneliness!

"I've rarely dared to say what I really thought so many times in life, without any consideration, without pleasing anyone, without hiding who I really am… how could my mom know what I felt if she was also taught to be a good girl who didn't express what was truly happening inside of her? It's a painful circle for which no one takes responsibility." Tears poured out of her eyes, and she stormed out.

Adam felt he was overstepping his educational role. In his mind he saw the silent man hugging the pillow, having given in to his mute soul, desperate from expressing himself among people and having been sent to the silent institution. Sadness spread within him and the guilt of responsibility gripped him, until he had to leave class and calm her down.

On his way to her, he started feeling the extraordinary movement of her soul, which he certainly liked as it allowed her to rise above her early habits in exposing her gentle soul, without knowing whether it would be greeted with fierceness or loving tenderness.

Stifled sounds of loss humbly emerged from her, and Adam sat next to her, helpless and silent for several long minutes until she turned to him with crying eyes and said: “I remember how you said in front of everyone that you’re lonely too, how you explained that I should tell the truth despite everything. I can’t believe how relieved we all were to see someone like you express such painful honesty. I still couldn’t feel it myself after you said it. Only now, after being able to openly express what I think and hurt, encountering myself through the eyes of other people in the world, only now can I truly feel myself. This experience makes me happy. Thanks to that I can discover other parts of my soul, and feel great pain for the many years that passed until I agreed to really be present in my world rather than just being there.”

Adam looked into the girl’s eyes with wonder mixed with jealousy, for the sensitivity of her thoughts as someone who could act in actual life and not just pick its wounds as a pleasuring addiction.

“I now see how hard it is for you to carry these complex emotions in one breath within you, but know that the words you’ve expressed were a brief education on your influence upon all those around you. You poured the courage of rebellion into their hearts so they could be independent without hiding or being ashamed. Maybe each of us will now agree to be a bit more ourselves.”

Relaxed breaths filled her lungs with an embracing silence. Her eyes seemed like they were processing the last hour, until she got up and thanked Adam for not leaving her alone in those moments. “It might hurt a lot right now, but I feel an inner power burning within me that I’ve never felt before. I’m excited to finally be feeling my soul.”

These simple words that seemed to erupt from her unplanned were the fault line of her soul, still unable to appreciate the consequences of this event.

Her innocent words constantly played, hammering him as if exposing a well-kept blind spot, one that seldom emerged as a feeling yet could still not be put into words.

His hands rested on his head. He closed his eyes, preparing for an internal conversation with bustling voices so he could savor those last moments in his heart.

I've dealt with cellars of solitude and forgetfulness for so many years, terrified of losing my memories and the few people I could be with in a loving presence. The anxieties of recent times signaled to me just how much effort I was putting into attempting to control my emotions, and how much this attempt has narrowed the experience of my existence to helpless surrender. So many words burst from my soul, stiflingly being pulled into that same whirlpool of existence in which it tries to overcome life's limitations.

What else do I have left, other than looking at this life with gentle compassion? I felt firsthand that within my anxieties to forget were all of my loves as well. In all my pain I've found that I'm a loving man, afraid of losing the testaments of my soul. I've nothing left but to admit that the constant touch of nullifying danger allows me to feel my soul powerfully, over and over again – a thing that was denied me as a child, when I had to push my feelings deep down without expressing them, without shouting out what had happened to me.

It now seems my hands aren't letting go of their firm grip on my pain, since it's so exciting to express the range of my emotions, my secret cries that were never heard. No one will prevent that of me.

I have no choice but to admit that melancholy is also an expression of love.

Lightning Source UK Ltd.
Milton Keynes UK
UKHW020738190123
415610UK00014B/1631